Monsters
and
Water Beasts

Creatures of Fact or Fiction?

Karen Miller

with illustrations by Sergio Ruzzier

HENRY HOLT AND COMPANY
New York

To my husband, Bob, and my children
Amy, Bobby, Dan, and Andrew

To my mother, Emily Jane, and my father, Emil,
who read to me

—K. M.

Henry Holt and Company, LLC
Publishers since 1866
175 Fifth Avenue
New York, New York 10010
www.henryholtchildrensbooks.com

Henry Holt® is a registered trademark of Henry Holt and Company, LLC.
Text copyright © 2007 by Karen Miller
Illustrations copyright © 2007 by Sergio Ruzzier
All rights reserved.
Distributed in Canada by H. B. Fenn and Company Ltd.

Library of Congress Cataloging-in-Publication Data
Miller, Karen.
Monsters and water beasts: creatures of fact or fiction? /
Karen Miller; with illustrations by Sergio Ruzzier.—1st ed.
p.   cm.
ISBN-13: 978-0-8050-7902-9
ISBN-10: 0-8050-7902-5
1. Sea monsters. 2. Mermaids. I. Ruzzier, Sergio. II. Title.
GR910.M55 2007   398.24'54—dc22   2006019663

First Edition—2007 / Designed by Laurent Linn
Printed in China on acid-free paper. ∞

1 3 5 7 9 10 8 6 4 2

CONTENTS

INTRODUCTION

There are many more living species on earth than we've yet discovered. While most of the unnamed species will probably turn out to be beetles less than a quarter inch long, something much bigger may be waiting.

As long as men have sailed the seas, there have been stories of sea serpents. The accounts tell of giant tentacles reaching out of the sea and dragging down men and boats. Most doubted these tales. Then, in 2002, a squid carcass over 50 feet long, longer than most whales, washed up on a Tasmanian beach. In September 2005, a living specimen in the North Pacific was documented on film. Because it lives at depths of over 3,000 feet, the giant squid has eluded capture for thousands of years.

Should we take stories of the cadborosaurus seriously? Pictures of the sea beast have been found in prehistoric caves on the coast of America and Canada. Tourists and locals believe they've spotted the beast swimming along the shores of British Columbia. It's hard to say.

The hairy beast Bigfoot has been seen by people all over the world. In Tibet and China he is called the yeti, in the Pacific Northwest he is known as Sasquatch, and in the Peruvian Andes people call him the ucu. Is it possible that Bigfoot will be the next beast to move from myth to reality?

We cannot know how many more intriguing creatures hinted at in myth and legend wait to be discovered. We do know, however, that science will continue to search. Some creatures may always remain mythical. But if history is any guide, some might one day wash up on the shore or walk out of the forest.

MONSTERS

BIGFOOT

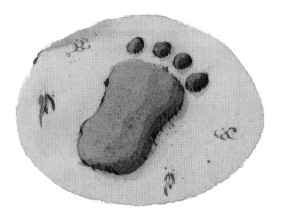

One spring day in 1924 Albert Ostman set off to find a gold mine. He pitched his tent in a sun-dappled clearing surrounded by tall trees. It was the perfect place for a campsite, at least until the second night. That night Albert awoke from a sound sleep as something yanked him, sleeping bag and all, out of the tent. His captor pushed his way through the woods, bumping and slamming through the trees with Albert concealed in his sleeping bag. Finally, the creature dumped Albert on the ground. He peeked over the top of his sleeping bag. There, just a few feet away, stood four beasts. They were at least seven feet tall and covered with hair.

Terrified, Albert waited for an attack, but it didn't come. The beasts treated him kindly, giving him berries, nuts, and greens to eat. They let him take things from his supply bag whenever he needed.

Soon it became obvious that the beasts wanted to keep Albert, for the old male guarded the only exit out of the valley. Albert decided to use the beast's curiosity in a plan for escape. One night he offered the elder beast a bit of snuff. The beast seemed to like it and consumed the contents of an entire can. After he finished, he fell to the ground. He rocked back and forth and made low, whistling moans. While the rest of the family watched the male, Albert grabbed his rifle and ran. He raised his gun and fired a warning shot to discourage a chase. The family, even the distressed male, scattered into the trees.

Albert ran until he stumbled across a group of loggers. He told them he had become lost while looking for a gold mine. He didn't tell them about his encounter. In fact, he kept the story a secret for thirty-three years. After all, who would believe him? It was only after reading news reports about other Bigfoot sightings that he decided to tell his tale. Albert's initial fear proved correct: Everyone laughed at him. It wasn't until twenty years later that some experts took him seriously.

The Creature: Big Feet, Big Body, and a Very Big Smell

The imprint of the creature's foot earned him his first American nickname, Bigfoot. According to Bigfoot believers, the print measured 14 to 18 inches in length and was 7 inches wide. Bigfoot's feet were unusual in other ways as well. His toes lined up like peas in a pod, and he was missing one toe, the big toe that humans have.

Everything else about Bigfoot was big, too. Adult males were described as 7 to 9 feet tall and weighing between 300 and 800 pounds. They all had large barrel-shaped chests and arms that hung lower than a human's.

Although his head was small and pointed, Bigfoot was no dimwit. He was brighter than most mammals,

and used a shriek-whistle to communicate with others of his kind.

A nocturnal animal, he made his home where there was an adequate supply of water and forest cover. He usually inhabited caves, forest nests, or abandoned buildings. Although he relied mostly on foraged fruits and vegetables, he was known to eat small rodents. No one had seen him using tools or making fire, so he seemed to behave like an animal, not a human, in his food gathering and eating.

About 10 percent of the reports (there are more than 2,600) tell of Bigfoot's strong odor. He smelled, to civilized noses, like someone who never washed. Sulfur, rotten eggs, and vomit were all words used to describe the stench.

Where did Bigfoot come from? Believers had an idea, the Bigfoot-Giganto theory. In 1935, a paleontologist, a scientist who studies fossil remains, found some unusual teeth in a Chinese pharmacy. These fossilized teeth, he determined, came from an animal that lived 6.3 million years ago. When jawbones were later discovered, scientists reconstructed the creature named the *Gigantopithecus*. This breed of powerful apes inhabited southern Asia. They lived alongside

Homo erectus, our human ancestor. *Homo erectus* learned how to use fire and tools, but the *Gigantopithecus* ape did not. Paleontologists have not been able to find the bones of the *Gigantopithecus* in Asia. Some think the genus died out. Others think the race of apes moved away. They believe *Gigantopithecus* traveled over the land bridge of the Bering Strait, just as the ancestors of our Native Americans are thought to have done. Believers say that the *Gigantopithecus* found a home in America, as the Indians did, and has never left.

Fact or Fancy: Now You See Him . . . Now You Don't

Bigfoot has been spotted all over the world. In the last two hundred years, he has been sighted in eleven foreign countries, nine Canadian provinces, and in every state in the U.S. except Hawaii. The first photographic evidence of Bigfoot didn't come until 1967. It was then that the Bigfoot film made its debut.

Reportedly filmed while Roger Patterson and a fellow Bigfoot hunter were horseback riding, the film showed Bigfoot walking away from the camera. For a time many people accepted this film as the first real proof that Bigfoot existed. However, Dr. John Napier, a primatologist (a scientist who studies apes and monkeys), said the movie was a hoax. He thought the animal moved like a human in a gorilla suit.

Other experts disagreed with Dr. Napier. They studied the creature's muscles in the Patterson video and said they exhibited real muscle movement. In 1997, the British Broadcasting Company presented a movie in which they attempted to debunk the Patterson film. Using the same film technology available in 1967, they re-created the encounter. Unfortunately, the BBC film's Bigfoot had bright red fur, not a shade ever reported in a North American Bigfoot. Also, the arms of the BBC Bigfoot were about the same length as a human's. The Patterson Bigfoot, however, had unusually long arms, nothing like that of a human. So, their effort to expose the hoax wasn't very convincing.

Dr. Napier's dismissal of the Patterson tape didn't stop him from studying Bigfoot further. In 1970, a set of strange footprints was discovered in the snow in Washington State. Dr. Napier examined the footprint casts (1,089 in all) and determined that they were made by a crippled, possibly clubfooted, Bigfoot. Other tracks have been found in isolated sites all over the world.

But pranksters can make tracks, too. In 2002, the Ray Wallace family revealed that their father had been leaving Bigfoot tracks in the American Northwest. Ray left his first set of footprints in 1958, using a pair of sixteen-inch carved wooden feet. With those and others of different sizes, he was able to fool people for many years. Scientists, therefore, need more evidence that Bigfoot tracks are genuine.

One of the most unusual reports about Bigfoot has revealed possible physical evidence. In 1976, something tried to force its way into a home in Washington State. The family woke to the sounds of breaking glass. Leaping out of bed and grabbing his rifle, the father ran to the storage room. It was empty, but bloody glass and bits of hair lay on the floor. The blood and hair were sent to a laboratory to determine exactly what had broken into their house. The results were uncertain. They said the blood came from a high primate and that the hair was similar to a gorilla's. However, the hair was not from a gorilla or from any other known primate.

Why haven't more people taken pictures of Bigfoot? Supporters answer that Bigfoot knows to stay out of sight. He forages for food after sunset. Also, he makes his home in remote, rural areas. If one does spy a Bigfoot, there usually isn't time to focus and shoot. Most encounters end as soon as Bigfoot senses a human. Also, if Bigfoot does exist, why haven't his bones been found? This might be explained by studying animal behavior. Large mammals often retreat to hiding places when ill or wounded to elude hungry predators. Bigfoot may use the same escape plan to avoid man and his camera.

Recent Sightings: Bigfoot Believers Band Together

Notable scientists have added their support to the existence of Bigfoot. In 2002, Jane Goodall, the respected chimpanzee researcher, surprised many people during an interview on National Public Radio. She said that she believed in the existence of large, undiscovered primates, such as the yeti or Sasquatch. A professor of anatomy and anthropology at Idaho State University, Jeff Meldrum, explained why a 400-pound plaster cast helped prove Bigfoot was real. The impression, made in the fall of 2000, had been found in Bigfoot country, in southwest Washington State, where a good many sightings have been reported over the years. The cast was made from an impression set in mud when the animal lay down to pick fruit. It left behind imprints of a heel, Achilles tendon, buttocks, thigh, and forearm. It was much bigger than a human—40 to 50 percent bigger—and its anatomy was unlike any known creature.

Every year, eyewitnesses and scientists meet to sift through new information. In October 2003, the police in northwest Arkansas were flooded with calls telling of an apelike animal roaming the area. The police took the stories seriously enough to ask the witnesses to contact them with more information. In 2005, there were more than twenty-seven sightings across the United States. A man in Kentucky saw a Bigfoot-like creature on a local road, as did a California motorist.

Many Native Americans have objected to the ridicule heaped on Bigfoot, for they consider him to be a brother to all mankind. Each tribe has its own word for Bigfoot—Salish, Seeahtik, and Sasquatch are a few. Native Americans count more than two hundred Bigfoot stories and point to five-thousand-year-old Bigfoot petroglyphs (carvings or line drawings in ancient caves) to support their belief.

The Indians of the Northwest used masks, carved in the image of local animals, for their ceremonies. Though the bear, wolf, and raven were the most commonly seen, Bigfoot was also represented. There was the mask of the Dzoonokwa, a heavy-browed, hairy creature that stole children. Two British Columbia tribes, the Tsimshian and the Nisga, used a human-ape mask. A Nootka mask most resembled Bigfoot. Its brow and chin were sloped, and the nose was short and flat. The lips were pursed as if ready to whistle.

Some think the Bigfoot's shrill cry is more than a primitive communication. They say Bigfoot came to tell us to take better care of the earth, for he is a friend to both man and the land. So if one hears the Bigfoot whistle, listen carefully.

The Big Bird of Texas

It was early in the morning on January 1, 1976, the first day of a new year and too nice to stay inside. Jackie and Tracey skipped outside to blue skies, open fields, and a whole day without school. Yet as the cousins stood in the yard, they felt uneasy. It was too still, too quiet. The sound, when it came, made them jump.

"*Eeee!*" shrieked an enormous bird less than a hundred yards away. The cousins ran into the house for a pair of binoculars, half hopeful that the creature would fly away before they returned outside. It did not.

The bird was over five feet tall with big red eyes and large wings folded close to its body. Tracey focused the binoculars on the face. Its beak, sharp and thick, projected down six inches over its odd, apelike face.

A few moments later, the creature was gone. Then suddenly it stood close to them, its head peeking over a small clump of trees. Jackie and Tracey didn't wait for it to come closer. They scrambled back through the door and stayed inside for the rest of the morning. When their parents awakened, the girls told them about the bird monster. Jackie's stepfather checked the yard and surrounding field. That was when he saw the tracks. They were pressed an inch and a half into the hard, sunbaked ground.

At first, no one believed the accounts, but soon there were so many sightings that the media changed its mind. They named the monster Big Bird, in honor of the popular character on *Sesame Street*.

The big bird was seen all over the Texas Rio Grande Valley. Neighbors, policemen, and teachers, whose word and reputations were respected, said they had seen it, too. Seven weeks after its arrival, the big bird swooped over three schoolteachers on their way to work. As soon as they got to school, they rushed to the library and found a picture of what they had seen. It was a creature who had lived over sixty million years ago. A pterosaur.

The Creature: Pleistocene Relic

Although accounts varied, many described a kind of pterosaur. These reptiles, which lived at the same time as dinosaurs, were the first flying animals with backbones. Once up in the air, they flew by gliding, not by flapping their wings. This was what many of the eyewitnesses reported. The big bird did not flap its 15-to-20-foot wings like a bird; it floated on air currents. People said they could almost see a skeleton move under its skin as it soared overhead.

At rest, the big bird was just as imposing as in flight. Standing five feet tall, it folded its wings like a bat and made high-pitched noises. Its throat quivered as it screeched out an earsplitting *"eeee!"* The thick beak dominated the bird's face, which some said looked like a gorilla and others a bat. None could forget the bird's eyes—eyes that were the size of silver dollars and glowed ember red.

The big bird's tracks differed in size, though the shape was the same. Each imprint showed one end as squared and the other three-toed, and measured between 8 and 10 inches. Everyone who saw the tracks agreed that the big bird was indeed big. Based on the impression the creature's feet made in the ground, its weight was estimated to be over 160 pounds.

Fact or Fancy: Winged Reptile or All-American Bird?

The witnesses had seen something, authorities concluded. But had their imaginations added snouts and leathery skin to ordinary birds? Zoologists thought the bird was likely a white pelican or great blue heron. Police sightings of the big bird did seem like those of a white pelican, not a relic from dinosaur days. Early morning light and mist might have made the pelican's normal 10-foot wingspan seem to be the 15-foot wingspan reported. The bendable neck could have been a pelican's neck, one that retracted as it flew. It was actually a great blue heron that fifty people fled from one February day, not the big bird. Only after the creature, filmed by a news reporter, was identified as a local bird did hysteria stop.

The false sightings could suggest that some people made mistakes because they were too excited. After all, the white pelican and the great blue heron look nothing like the big birds reported by others.

What of reports of a pterosaur? Most dismissed this as ridiculous, until 1972, when scientists found pteranodon fossils in Big Bend National Park. The pteranodon, a member of the pterosaur family, lived more than sixty million years ago. It had a wingspan of about 50 feet and was so large that it couldn't fly in the normal way. Scientists think it must have launched itself from nearby cliffs and then glided through the air.

Many people live in the Rio Grande Valley. How could such a species exist without being detected? The International Society of Cryptozoology, a group that investigates reports of unknown or extinct animals, proposes an answer. Sightings of the big bird occur only 200 miles east of one of the most unexplored, unknown areas in North America, the Sierra Madre mountains of Mexico. Perhaps the big bird is nesting there.

Other Sightings:
Has the Big Bird Flown the Coop?

The big bird himself has not been seen in Texas for many years. In fact, the last mass sighting was reported in the Rio Grande Valley over twenty years ago. However, in other parts of the world, giant winged creatures continue to fly overhead. Giant birds have been reported all over the United States, from San Francisco to Pennsylvania. The accounts tell of a dark creature with a large wingspan. In New Guinea, tales of the ropen come from the locals, the U.S. military, missionaries, and field researchers. The ropen is identified as having strong wings, a tail with a flange, and a beak filled with sharp teeth. In northern Zimbabwe, the locals talk of a flying reptilelike beast. It is considered dangerous, for it attacked people and capsized boats. Its aggression earned it a nickname, the kongomato, or "breaker of boats." The kongomato has leathery wings that unfold to a length of 4 to 7 feet. It has the perfect escape route—the Jiunda swamp. The swamp stretches for miles and miles. Once in the deep, dense swamp, the kongomato can lose even the best hunter. Another pterosaur-type predator, called the olitu, "overwhelmer of boats," has been spotted in the neighboring country of Zambia.

Did a flying reptile, a descendant of the pterosaur, leave its lair in Mexico and fly over the border to Texas? Or was the big bird sighted just an ordinary bird, like a great blue heron or white pelican? Possibly, to find our answer, all we have to do is wait.

Hoop Snakes

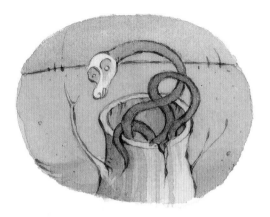

As legend has it, three woodsmen went into the Georgia woods to cut timber. They worked until the sun slipped down past the treetops. As they stacked their last pile, Oldest Brother saw a tree they had missed. He took his ax and with one whack split the oak in two. The tree fell with a swish instead of a crash.

"It's a hollow tree," he said. "What a surprise!"

A bigger surprise slithered out from the hollow oak: a long black snake. It wasn't any of the poisonous snakes they knew, but the brothers decided not to take any chances.

Youngest Brother grabbed his ax and chopped off its head. Satisfied, the men began chopping the oak into firewood. They had been working for only a few minutes when Middle Brother saw another black snake.

Before they could raise their axes, the snake whipped past them up the hill. It shot through the underbrush, winding in and around the trees, all the way to the top. What happened next made them drop their axes and run for their lives.

At the crest of the hill, the snake stopped, put its tail in its mouth, and popped up into a vertical position. It rolled slowly at first, then picked up speed. By the time it reached the bottom of the hill, it clipped along as fast as the brothers. The men split up as they dashed through the woods. The snake kept rolling head-over-tail through the underbrush, getting closer with each roll to Youngest Brother.

Youngest Brother darted in and out of the trees, hoping to confuse the snake. Then he stopped, turned, and waited. At just the right moment, he hunkered down and threw himself through the hoop snake.

The startled snake ran right into a young cottonwood tree. Its stinger tail whipped out of its mouth and stuck in the bark. The snake was trapped.

The men walked over to their brother and picked him up. Together, they examined the tree. Snake venom seeped down the trunk, and the little sapling began to swell. It ballooned and bulged until it was the size of an older tree. One by one, the leaves withered and fell. The sapling turned to a pale shade of green, the color of the snake's venom.

Oldest Brother dispatched the snake with his ax while Middle Brother took down the tree. Quickly, they loaded the green wood onto their wagon. Youngest Brother didn't say a word, for he was shaking too hard to speak. Congratulating themselves, the brothers headed out of the forest. They had managed to outsmart the Southern hoop snake.

The Creature: A Hoop with a Deadly Sting

Some say the hoop snake is the most dangerous snake in the South. Rattlesnakes warn away people with their rattles, and water moccasins and copperheads are so slow that even a child could get away from them. The hoop snake, with its deadly and silent approach, is a match for the fastest runner.

Hoop snakes have been described as being black as well as multicolored. They measure about 8 feet long and are small in diameter. In fact, they resemble a rolling hula hoop in their size and shape. The head of the hoop snake is like any other snake, but its tail is sharp, with a stinger on its end. The hoop snake can safely hold its tail in its mouth. The stinger ranges from 1 to 5 inches long. About a half-inch from the stinger is a valve that shoots poison. If stung, a person dies within minutes.

There are two ways to avoid a hoop snake sting. The first is to run uphill. The snake can only roll down, not up, a hill, so it will have to slither along. Eventually it tires and gives up the chase. Or one can jump through the rolling snake's hoop and confuse it. Then the snake will run into something else and most likely sink its tail into a tree or fence post.

Fact or Fancy: Can the Hoop Snake Roll?

Are there really hoop snakes? Herpetologists, scientists who study snakes, are doubtful. They haven't

seen a snake roll down a hill and believe a snake's body can't hold the shape of a hoop. They think the story of the hoop snake originated with actual reports of a mud snake. The mud snake is usually found lying in a loose coil on the ground. It has a hard spine and sharp tail. Because of the horny scales and stiff spine, it might draw blood if flailed against one's skin. When it is picked up, it uses its tail to feel about. Since the tail is sharp, it might prick, but it shouldn't pierce the skin. The mud snake, though, is not the hoop snake of stories. When threatened, the mud snake doesn't roll into a hoop. It slides away like most other snakes. Believers say this only proves that the mud snake is not the real hoop snake.

Recent Sightings: Outside the Door!

While most common in the South, hoop snake tales turn up all across the United States, from Pennsylvania to Washington State, and stories of the hoop snake are common in other parts of the world, like Australia, where cyclists watch out for the rolling reptile. In 2005, a Texas woman reported seeing a hoop snake rolling in the desert. This time, no harm was meant, for the hoop snake did not pursue her. A herpetologist heard a startling and different story back in 2001. A rolling snake had chased a man all the way to his back door. A moment after he slammed the door, he heard a thump. The man peeked out the door, only to see the snake's tail disappear under his house.

It's hard to say if hoop snakes exist. Sightings are consistently reported, and herpetologists actually discuss hoop snakes in state and national park publications. They explain why the so-called hoop snakes are really sidewinder rattlesnakes (in the Southwest) or different kinds of mud snakes (on the East Coast, in the Midwest, and in Australia). Perhaps it's better not to take any chances. If there's talk of a snake in the neighborhood, hope that it's not a hoop snake. If it is, remember there are only two ways to escape it. You can run past the snake back up the hill or—if you are as bold as the woodsman—jump through its hoop!

MOTHMAN

One November night in 1966, two couples drove to the TNT dump, a favorite hangout for the young people of Point Pleasant, West Virginia. Used as an ammunition and explosive (TNT) base during World War II, the site had been returned to an animal preserve. The two couples expected to meet friends and cruise the abandoned roads. That night, though, they didn't meet their friends, they met Mothman.

The creature appeared without warning in front of

their car, its eyes glowing red in the headlights. The group froze, for the creature's eyes seemed to have hypnotic power. Finally, the monster turned and shuffled away.

It wasn't gone for long. As they sped off, they saw the creature's large eyes behind them. Just as their car reached city limits, the creature rose into the air and flew toward them. It squeaked and shrieked as it caught up to their car. They couldn't outpace the creature even though they sped along at a hundred miles per hour.

They weren't the only ones to see Mothman that night. Five more people called the police station with reports of a strange birdlike creature.

The sheriff called a press conference. The conference was held to warn the townspeople, but it also sent Mothman into the airwaves. Within days, the story had spread across America, and reporters gave the creature its name.

The sightings of Mothman multiplied as days passed. Unusual electric and telephone troubles plagued the town, and animals disappeared. After the locals began reporting strange lights in the sky, UFO enthusiasts came calling. Reports that men in black (MIB) were canvassing neighborhoods and asking about Mothman flooded the police station. The townspeople were frightened. Was there an alien in their midst?

Thirteen months after the first report, a tragedy befell the town. The town's bridge over the Ohio River collapsed, killing forty-six people. Since that happened, Mothman has not been seen in Point Pleasant. Did the creature have something to do with the catastrophe? No one knows for sure.

The Creature: No Head, No Neck, but What a Pair of Wings!

Mothman stood about 7 feet tall. The creature was broader than an ordinary man and seemed to weigh about 200 pounds. In fact, it looked little like a man, even though it had a humanoid shape. Its outer skin was dark and scaly, and it was missing a neck. Two phosphorescent eyes topped the trunk. Folded against the back were two batlike wings, but no one ever saw them flap. When Mothman left a scene, it rose straight up, opening its large wings to catch an updraft. Witnesses noted a mechanical humming or high squeaking noise as it flew.

Fact or Fancy: Is It a Bird, a Curse, or an Alien?

Where did Mothman come from? Suggestions are wild and wide-ranging. Some suspect Mothman was an alien. Others said Mothman was the instrument of an old Indian curse. A third group said Mothman was possibly a bird.

UFO believers claimed the town's bridge collapse was proof that Mothman had been an alien, for what other than an extraterrestrial could buckle and snap steel supports? It was a terrible and unexpected event, others agreed, but instead they laid the blame with Chief Cornstalk, an Indian chief who had been murdered by local settlers almost two hundred years earlier. Before he died, he promised tragedy for the people and their land. The engineers who examined the bridge didn't find an otherworldly cause, however. They found the bridge to be poorly designed, poorly maintained, and unable to carry the weight of modern cars. So Mothman as a catalyst of doom, either from this world or out of it, was dismissed by experts.

Was Mothman a result of chemical spills in the TNT preserve? Even though the munitions factory was abandoned after the war, the army left behind storage facilities. Perhaps a harmful substance leaked into the groundwater, affecting the local animal population. Could Mothman have been a mutated bird?

Biologists say Mothman was no mutation, just an ordinary bird. The barn owl, they explained, has many Mothman features. An owl's flight is noiseless, and its large eyes reflect red when illuminated. The owl, too, has no neck. Yet there are no barn owls as tall as Mothman, or as noisy in flight.

Another bird suggested is the sandhill crane, which stands 4 to 6 feet high. The crane is an aggressive bird that has been known to run or fly after people. Although not native to the area, a flock of sandhill cranes had been spotted only seventy miles from town. But wildlife rangers in Point Pleasant had not seen any cranes. Another drawback to this theory is the way the crane flies. When it lifts into the air, it flaps its wings. According to reports, Mothman never flapped its wings on takeoff. It seemed to lift up and away.

Recent Sightings: Mothman's Vanishing Act

Flying humanoids continue to be seen all over the world. Two years after the bridge collapse in Point Pleasant, a bird-woman fluttered in front of a Marine guard in Danang, Vietnam. In that same year, a creature described as an owl man flew over and around the village of Hampshire, England.

Recently, flying beings were reported on the Indonesian island of Ceram. The orang-bati, as the creature was called, was reported to carry off animals and young children. About five feet tall with black leathery wings and blood-red skin, it left its cave at night to hunt. Although initially skeptical, some missionaries who heard the villagers' stories came to believe in the creature.

There were over a hundred sightings of Mothman in Point Pleasant. Did the people see a common bird, an alien, or a true monster? It remains a mystery.

THE JERSEY DEVIL

Late at night in the Pine Barrens of New Jersey, a ten-year-old boy sat up in bed. Something was screaming outside his window. It wasn't a squawk or a whistle. It began on a high note that hurt his ears. Then it dropped down so low he could barely hear it. It was a sad and horrible sound. The boy lifted the curtain and scanned the pine trees. That's when he saw the monster. It hopped and flew on a diagonal line

across the yard until it stood directly beneath him. When he got a look at it, he gasped, for its face was streaked with blood. The beast tilted its head as if listening and sniffed the air. It shrieked one more time, then unfurled its wings and flew away. It was 1951, and the Jersey Devil was back in town.

The police were suspicious about the calls they received. Over the years, many people had claimed to have seen the Jersey Devil. Actually, in 1909, when a ten-thousand-dollar award was offered for its capture, two men had boasted that they actually owned one. Jacob Hope and Norman Jeffries said they had snared the monster while on a trip to Australia. Their beast, which they identified as an Australian vampire, had escaped when they were crossing the Pine Barrens. As proof, they presented it to the public. It was a kangaroo with glued-on claws, wings, and painted stripes. They didn't fool anyone.

Suspicious or not, the police investigated. During the 1951 sightings, they followed one set of tracks and found a stick attached to a stuffed bear paw. Investigators thought they had solved the mystery, even though the creature was reported to have hooves for feet, not

paws. They posted signs all over town—"The Jersey Devil Is a Hoax." Not everyone believed them. People still heard screams in the pine woods. Family pets went missing and livestock disappeared. As time went on, fewer and fewer reports trickled in. The Jersey Devil eventually lost the last of its frightening reputation when it became the mascot and name of a New Jersey hockey team.

The Creature: Monster of Many Faces

According to legend, several hundred years ago a woman named Mother Leeds had twelve children. She was so poor that she had to rely on handouts and kindnesses to care for her family. When she discovered she was going to have another child, Mother Leeds said she was tired of children. "Let this one be the devil!" She got her wish. When the child was first born, it was a sweet baby boy. But as she held him in her arms, he began to change. The little feet became hooves, the round head lengthened into a horselike shape, and bat wings sprouted from his shoulder blades. Mother Leeds dropped him and clapped her

hands to her mouth. She watched him transform into a creature the size of a small man. Horrified, Mother Leeds drove him from her home.

The Jersey Devil returned again and again, each time hoping his mother would take him in. Even after Mother Leeds passed away, he continued to roam the countryside of the Pine Barrens, heartbroken.

Descriptions of the Jersey Devil varied. Some said the face looked like a hideous kangaroo, others said he looked like a German shepherd. One witness claimed the creature's head did have a horse face, but its size was small, like a collie's. Most agreed on the body. A long, thin neck supported the head, and the creature stood about four feet tall. It had four skinny legs, with the two front legs short, like those of a *Tyrannosaurus rex*. The feet were shaped like hooves and made distinctive horselike tracks in the ground. His leathery wings were about two feet long and allowed him to jump onto roofs and into trees. He seemed to be a carnivore, for chickens and other small farm animals vanished whenever the creature was spotted.

Fact or Fancy: What Is the Jersey Devil's Real Shape?

How could a monster exist in a state as crowded as New Jersey and not be discovered, caught, and examined? Fans of the Jersey Devil explain that while much of the state is filled with people and industry, the Jersey Devil's home in the barrens is not. Few people live there because work is so scarce. The land can't be farmed, and the mines for iron ore are depleted. There are over a million acres of sandy pine forests and primeval swamp. Two minutes after leaving a road, one could wander in a thicket of ghostly white pines or sink into a bog.

People who believe in the Jersey Devil point out that the Pine Barrens is a place where odd things happen. The Lenni Lenape tribe, who first lived in the barrens, would not hunt in certain areas, even though game abounded there. Many think of the barrens as an otherworldly place and tell tales of rumrunners, pirates, and Mafia massacres. The *Hindenburg* dirigible, said to be the safest gas-powered blimp of its time, exploded and crashed in the Pine Barrens. When the movie producers of two horror films, *The Blair Witch*

Project (1999) and *The Exorcist* (1973), needed eerie settings, they chose the Pine Barrens.

The Jersey Devil has the reputation of causing bad luck. From the Civil War to the Vietnam War, the creature appeared just before hostilities began. In 1939, families in Mount Holly were startled awake by the sound of hooves clattering on their roofs. World War II began soon after in Europe. It seemed as if a crop failure followed whenever the Jersey Devil appeared.

Skeptics point out that the Jersey Devil is a convenient excuse to explain misfortune or to stir up excitement. In the early 1950s, teenagers spotted the Jersey Devil and mass hysteria spread from one town to another. Visitors from all over the East Coast swarmed the barrens to help hunt for it.

Zoologists say the answer to the Jersey Devil can be found by looking in a book. Turn to the page with the sandhill crane, they say, and see the similarities between the two. Sandhill cranes have long, thin legs and give a shrill screeching cry. The cranes seem to fly on a diagonal line, almost as if they are heading into a crosswind. Also, the birds will attack if they are approached. Cranes, too, are about 4 feet tall (the estimated size of the Jersey Devil).

There is even an explanation for the Mother Leeds story. Mother Leeds, say some, probably did exist. She most likely gave birth to a deformed child whom she hid away in her house. As the child grew older, so did Mother Leeds. Eventually, Mother Leeds sickened and could no longer care for her child. He was forced to forage the countryside and raid neighboring farms for food. Perhaps a hungry child is the root of all the stories.

Still, most in the Pine Barrens won't let go of the Jersey Devil. A sandhill crane doesn't have a horse's head or kill chickens. Until they know for sure, people in the barrens run inside and lock their doors if they hear a high-pitched whistle or a rustle of leathery wings.

Other Sightings: The Jersey Devil Hops, Jumps, and Flies Across the States

January 16 through 23, 1909, was a week of terror. The Jersey Devil was seen not only in New Jersey but also in New York and Pennsylvania. The entire Pine Barrens shut down as search parties scoured the countryside for the beast. There were tracks everywhere, some marking leaps from the ground to the rooftops. Farmers locked themselves in their houses, and school was canceled. No monster was captured.

In 1966, the newspapers reported another story. A local farmer said his entire flock of chickens and his guard dogs had been killed. He was certain it was the work of the Jersey Devil. When he couldn't supply any hard evidence, the police dismissed it. After that, the police and newspapers ignored the Jersey Devil. In recent years, any reports have gone to Web sites devoted to the beast. For an area that is only 1,600 square miles (one quarter the size of New Jersey), five or six reports a year is surprising. Witnesses such as an ambulance driver, a Fort Dix soldier, and entire families have described encounters.

In the 260 years of the Jersey Devil's existence, more than two thousand people have claimed to have seen or heard him. Is it a real monster or one created from our imagination? It's hard to say.

WATER BEASTS

SEA MAIDEN OF BILOXI

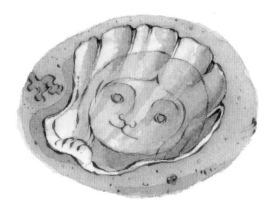

As long as the oldest grandfather could remember, the Mississippi Biloxi tribe had worshipped the river mermaid. On moonlit nights they walked to the banks of the Pascagoula to give thanks for their good fishing. The women of the tribe carried instruments for making music, and the men led the children. As the moon rose, so did the mermaid, and together they sang.

Legend has it that the Biloxi lived happily with their goddess until a missionary came. He told stories of plague and famine to convince them that his god was more powerful than theirs. He ordered them to destroy the mermaid's temple and statues. Frightened, the tribe pulled down the shrine and threw their carvings into the river. As the statues sank beneath the waves, the people watched in despair.

The next night the waters of the Pascagoula churned. The mermaid burst from the river and sang a song. Her voice floated through the trees to the village. No one could resist her call, and the village emptied. Once by the river, they laid logs on the fire until they had a towering blaze. They danced and chanted until dawn, when the mermaid sang again. This time she told of the watery delights in her realm at the bottom of the river. She called once more, and the tribe joined hands and jumped. When the sun rose moments later, not a single person remained.

No one knows what really happened to this Biloxi village. Another legend says the Biloxi, faced with certain defeat in battle against the Choctaw, marched into the river as a mass suicide. In 1700, French-Canadian explorer Pierre Le Moyne wrote about an abandoned Biloxi village on the Pascagoula. Not a single person remained in a town that had once been a center of fishing and trade. The Indian guides told Le Moyne that the people had died from something they could not fight—diseases of the white man. So the question remains unanswered. Yet those who have heard the river music disagree. The village may be gone, but on quiet nights the chants of the Biloxi can still be heard in the waters of the Pascagoula.

The Creature: A Temperamental Diva

Mermaids were mentioned in the first century when the Roman historian Pliny spoke of their mournful songs. From the beginning, they were both worshipped and feared. Some saw the mermaid as a monster, others as a beauty. All agreed, however, that a mermaid was half-human, half-fish. Today, most people think of Ariel, the Walt Disney company's sweet little mermaid. Or they visualize Hans Christian Andersen's fairy tale, where the mermaid gives her life for love. Reported accounts tell of a different kind of creature.

Although beautiful on the outside, many mermaids have been described as cruel and willful. They spent hours on rocks, preening, combing their shiny hair, and admiring their reflections in shell mirrors. Instead of rescuing drowning men, mermaids sank ships. Sometimes they used a lament to bring the soft-hearted sailors close. Other times they sang soul-snatching songs. If the day was windy and their song carried past the sailors, they gave their scent to the wind. Their natural perfume was as irresistible as their singing, so the men had no possibility of escape. As soon as the ship shattered on the rocks below, the mermaids stopped singing and waited. When one of the men made his way to their perch, they welcomed him with open arms. They droned him to sleep—and when the moment was right, they tore him apart with sharp green teeth.

Not all mermaids were vicious. It was said that many cared for the men and tried to live their lives with them. Those who wanted to stay on land donned a magic cap or cloak that made their fishtails disappear so they could walk the land and breathe the air. Others took the men under the sea to their homes. With mermaid magic, the sailors could live. That was no consolation for the men's loved ones, who were left behind on land. To them, the sailor was gone forever. In fact, spying a mermaid was considered an omen to a seaman. If he saw one, he knew he would soon disappear at sea.

Fact or Fancy: Is the Mermaid a Fish Story?

Are mermaids real? In the 1970s, an American anthropologist named Ray Wagner searched for a mermaid-like creature off the coast of New Guinea. The local people said the creature, called the ri, had a human head, arms, and torso. In fact, the ri looked like a woman, they reported. However, it didn't act like a lady. It seemed no smarter than any other fish. If the fishermen caught ri, they ate them. In 1985, a photo of a ri hit the newswires. Within moments, the New Guinea fishermen were proved correct. The ri had nothing of a woman in it. It was, in fact, a dugong.

Mainstream scientists think the mermaids were mistaken sightings of two types of marine mammals, pinnipeds and sirenians. A seal, dugong, sea cow, and manatee look human from afar because of their round eyes and flat faces. The pinniped seal and the sirenian manatee both rise out of the water like a human. The seal watches ships from an upright position, and so does the manatee when she nurses her young. Another reason for sightings may have been changes in the temperature of the sea surface. The effect of warm air moving over cold air causes refractions, or bendings, of the light rays. That, combined with the powerful emotion of homesickness, probably explains some sailors' reports of mermaids.

Yet, contend believers, if light and warm air distort the view, how can there have been so many intricate details in the reports? Men whose lives depended on how well they watched the sea could not make the mistake of thinking a sea creature was a woman. Also, three fourths of all mermaid sightings occur in waters where no manatees, dugongs, or seals swim.

Charlatans and pranksters hurt the case for mermaids. In the 1800s, Japanese fishermen created mermaids by attaching the top halves of monkeys to the bottom halves of fish. They sold the preserved remains to carnivals, museums, and the curious. In 2003, two Canadian girls dressed in mermaid costumes as a joke. For hours, they posed and preened on rocks off the shores of Acadia National Park in Maine.

Is there any possibility mermaids exist? Some say they are real but not the half-human creatures described. These people think mermaids are a sirenian species that has yet to be discovered. Others believe the mermaid is a descendant of an "aquatic ape." This theory, put forth by marine biologist Alistair Hardy in 1960 and popularized by writer Elaine Morgan in 1972, proposed that mankind's ancestors returned to the sea to live, just as whales did millions of years ago. When the aquatic ape returned to land to evolve into man, the merpeople remained in the water.

Perhaps mermaids did live long ago. Until this century, locals in northwest Scotland said the McVeagh clan was descended from merfolk. Families living on the Isle of Man in the Irish Sea were prey to mermaid charms, too. They believed their red hair was a gift from the mermaid side of the family. The Orkneys had a family trait—slightly webbed hands— that some claimed came from a selkie, a merperson who was half-seal, half-human and could shape-shift and shed its skin in order to walk on land.

Other Sightings:
Mermaids Swim into the Sunset

Despite ridicule over the years, sailors still report seeing mermaids. The Scottish Island of Muck has been the spot for many sightings, the most recent in 1947. An experienced fisherman checking boxes for lobster saw a mermaid twenty yards offshore. She sat combing her hair on the very lobster box he was about to haul in. As soon as she spied him, she slipped into the waves. No one could convince him that he had not seen a mermaid.

In September 1996, there was a sighting of a blond mermaid in Heavenly Lake, China. The mermaid played in the water for ten minutes and stirred waves six feet high before it disappeared underwater. The creature was spotted again in July 2005. This time, however, the head was black in color and the size of an adult ox.

In 1998, off the coast of Kona, Hawaii, a dive boat captain and fellow divers reported spotting a mermaid swimming with dolphins. An hour later, when the captain was underwater photographing fish, something brushed up against his leg. He looked down and saw a big speckled fin. The creature shot past him, heading for the surface. He pointed his camera and clicked. Is the image evidence? Or is it a computer-enhanced hoax? Many said the photo was too ambiguous to be taken as proof.

Will the Hawaiian mermaid make a reappearance? Could fossil remains of an aquatic ape lead to new theories about mermaids? It's hard to say what will be discovered in the ocean's deep, dark waters.

CHAMP

Sandy Mansi wanted to rest by the lake and watch her children play. While her husband retrieved his sunglasses and a camera from the car, she relaxed. The children waded and splashed, and Mrs. Mansi let her gaze glide over the water. Farther out on the lake, bubbles appeared on the surface. It was nothing unusual, but there was something odd about them. She watched as more and more bubbles surfaced.

Suddenly, a huge animal rose up out of the lake about 150 feet away. First she saw a small head, next a long graceful neck, and finally a brown humped back. It seemed to be 15 to 20 feet long. The creature looked like a prehistoric beast.

Mr. Mansi, returning from the car, saw the creature and called the children. He tossed the camera to Mrs. Mansi, who snapped a photo just before the animal sank out of sight. On that July day in 1977, Mrs. Mansi took the only authentic photo of Champ, the beast of Lake Champlain.

Afraid of looking foolish, the Mansis kept the photo in an album and showed it only to close friends and family. Soon the news spread, and eventually Roy Mackal, a biologist, and George Zug, a zoologist, examined it. The researchers sent it to a photographic expert to see if the photo had been retouched or changed. The expert declared the picture genuine. An oceanographer studied the waves in the photo and estimated the animal to be even larger than Mrs. Mansi described. He judged it to be more than 24 feet in length. Something big had definitely bubbled out of Lake Champlain.

The Creature:
A Zeuglodon or Plesiosaur?

From the beginning, the shape and size of Champ changed with each report. The first description of a monster in Lake Champlain was from the explorer Samuel de Champlain. His journal, however, did not describe the modern-day Champ. Champlain's report told of a large garfish, a primitive fish with sharp teeth and shiny, thick bony scales.

Most of the sightings before the 1970s were so vague that it was impossible to accurately identify Champ. A zeuglodon seemed the closest match for what witnesses described. A zeuglodon was an ancient whale, extremely long and snakelike in shape. It ate fish using jaws that contained two rows of teeth.

Reports since the 1970s showed Champ to be a ringer for the Loch Ness monster. Like Nessie, Champ had humps along his back and a small, horselike head. The body broadened out in the middle. Both monsters seemed similar to descriptions of a plesiosaur. The ancient plesiosaur was approximately 15 feet long, with a wide, fat body and a short tail. The neck was long and flexible. It swung its head side to side through schools of fish and chewed them up with its long, sharp teeth. The creature paddled through the water with large, paddle-shaped limbs.

Fact or Fancy: Does Champ Have a Secret Exit?

The Adirondack Mountains of New York State contain thick forests of pine, hemlock, and spruce that protect and hide its animals. So, contend Champ supporters, the region is the perfect hiding place for a monster.

Also, Champ's home, Lake Champlain, is not a typical lake. It was once part of the Atlantic Ocean. When glaciers ebbed ten thousand years ago, some of the ocean's waters and marine life became landlocked. There are those who say a reptile like the plesiosaur might have been trapped in the lake. If a mate had been trapped, too, the future of the monsters should have been assured.

Doubters find this argument unlikely. First, in order to have a breeding population, they say, there have to be at least fifty adults in the lake. This ensures that there are enough healthy animals to reproduce. There have to be at least five hundred animals to keep the population healthy for a long time.

Not true, counter Champ enthusiasts. Lake Champlain was connected to the Atlantic Ocean through underground rivers. So Champ and his family could travel by way of these waterways. They could feed in the ocean and stay out of sight.

Evidence already mentioned was the photo taken by Sandy Mansi. There are other eyewitness reports, too. Photo experts agreed that Mansi's photo was a real picture of something, but they couldn't be sure it was a lake monster. As for the sightings, the cynics say that logs, wind slicks, boat wakes, or a seiche (a single wave that moves back and forth between two shores of a lake) could look like a sea creature. Perhaps people saw the seiche roll across the lake and thought it was a monster swimming. Another factor in explaining a false sighting was sunlight. There were more reports just before sunset, when the light can play tricks with eyesight. Not so, argued a scientist who studied both Champ and the Loch Ness monster. If that were true, Nessie and Champ would be seen at the same time of day. Nessie, however, has been seen in the late morning or mid-afternoon hours, and Champ usually has been spotted just before sunset.

Recent Sightings: Reports Keep Rolling In

Avid fans of Champ have created Web sites where people can post reports. Each year, new reports emerge. In 1983, a woman photographed Champ swimming in Bulwagga Bay, New York. Her picture showed a dark object moving through the water. In 1994, a baby Champ was spotted. The baby was about eight feet long and left behind a wake as he swam past. The same person saw an adult Champ slap his neck back and forth across the surface of the water, stunning nearby fish. These events both occurred in the sunset hours, when fish surfaced to eat bugs that had accumulated during the day.

In 2000, when more than thirty eyewitness reports were filed, Champ was usually seen feeding. One video showed Champ with his head and neck out of the water. He appeared to be swallowing something, because his neck contracted in an up-and-down manner.

After a few minutes of feeding, he slipped under the waves. The photographic evidence hasn't been judged authentic, because the pictures were deemed grainy or too distant. Even the famous photograph taken by Mrs. Mansi has not been accepted as proof. While experts agree the photo is real and untouched, they don't know exactly where on the lake the picture was taken, and Mansi has not been able to help them. Evidence keeps coming in. *ABC News*, in February 2006, received a video of Champ filmed the previous summer. The tape showed a serpentlike creature swimming under the water, with a very strange wake. Two retired FBI analysts declared the tape unaltered but said it still wasn't clear enough to be considered proof.

The citizens of Vermont and New York were so worried about Champ that, in 1982, they passed laws to protect him. The Lake Champlain Land Trust, an organization that protects the lake's shores and waters, considers Champ to be a lake resident, even if he hasn't made an official appearance. Local residents are sure there is something big in the lake. Perhaps with the help of new electronic surveillance, Champ's fans will someday get to meet him.

THE SEA SERPENT
OF GLOUCESTER

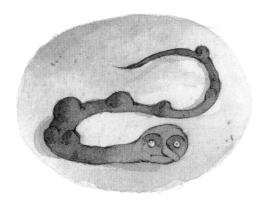

Matthew Gaffney stood in the bow of the boat, scanning the gray sea. His musket was loaded, and he and his fellow sailors were ready to shoot. It was 1817, and the sea serpent had returned to Massachusetts after an absence of almost two hundred years. Since the sixth of August, most everyone in Gloucester had seen the serpent once or twice. It was described as a giant snake with bumps on its back.

Matthew wondered if he would be able to hit the serpent. The rolling waves of the Atlantic rocked the boat, and the waters were deep and dark. Then, 30 yards away, a giant snake head arose from the sea. Matthew yelled, "Row!"

Slowly, they neared the beast, ready for attack. Sometimes the serpent moved forward, at other times it whipped its body around and wound itself in circles. It swam back and forth in the water, but not as a snake would. In fact, from a distance it resembled a line of bobbing buoys.

When Matthew was close enough, he lifted his gun. He fired directly into the monster's head. The serpent turned and looked, not appearing injured at all.

The monster made straight for the boat, then changed its mind and disappeared under the waves. Matthew and the others waited. They had seen whales splinter bigger boats than theirs, and this creature was at least 50 feet long. Sweat dripped from their foreheads, and they held their breath. Nothing happened.

"He's over there!" another sailor yelled. About a hundred yards away on the other side of the boat, the monster had resurfaced and was swimming in the opposite direction. The serpent was gone, but not for long.

The Creature: Three Parts Reptile and One Part Mammal

Although only 40 to 50 feet appeared above the water, the sea serpent of Gloucester was guessed to be about 65 feet long. Its body was as thick as a barrel and had a row of bumps, or humps, on the top. The rest of the serpent's body was smooth, like a snake's. The top was brownish-black, but a white stripe ran down its throat and belly.

The head was, as Matthew Gaffney noted, as big as a horse's head but flatter, so it looked more like a turtle, seal, or snake head.

The serpent was quick, swimming a mile in two or three minutes even though it moved up and down, like a caterpillar inching along. This up-and-down movement was a characteristic of mammals, not reptiles, confusing scientists as to its classification.

Fact or Fancy: Did Scientists Test the Real Monster?

The town of Gloucester was determined to solve the mystery of the sea serpent in a scientific way. Their justice of the peace took sworn accounts from witnesses, and a committee was formed to study the reports. A set of twenty-five questions was asked of everyone who saw the monster. Usually, people have different views of seeing something surprising. Yet in Gloucester everyone described the same monster.

Because the townspeople thought the serpent was a snake, they searched the beach for snake eggs. Soon two little boys found a three-foot-long black snake with humps down its back. Everyone was convinced that this was a baby sea monster. They named it *Scoliophis atlantis,* the Atlantic humped snake.

When the news and evidence of the serpent reached France, a scientist examined the tissues of the monster baby. He showed that it wasn't a sea serpent but a normal black snake with abnormal bumps.

The entire world laughed at Gloucester and its scientific committee. For a long time, no one spoke of any monster.

Even so, the next summer the same creature appeared off the coast of Maine. The summer after, the serpent returned to the shores of Massachusetts. In fact, it appeared every summer on the Atlantic coast for the next hundred years.

What had the people seen that afternoon in the harbor?

A scientist who studied lake and ocean creatures, Bernard Heuvelmans, said the Gloucester serpent was not a snake. A snake didn't move up and down when it swam; it moved from side to side. Heuvelmans was convinced that the spectators had seen a kind of plesiosaur. Its flippers allowed it to dive straight down in the water, as the sea serpent had been described as doing.

Paleontologist Robert Bakker had a different theory. Bakker believed the plesiosaur died off with the giant reptiles. Perhaps the sea serpent described was a prehistoric whale, a snakelike primitive whale called a zeuglodon.

Skeptics said the creature was not an ancient reptile or mammal, but a modern-day giant squid, which can grow longer than 50 feet. If a squid lifted one of its tentacles out of the water, it could resemble a long-necked sea monster.

What was it? We might never know. The investigation of the Gloucester sea serpent ended when the world laughed.

Recent Sightings:
The Unsinkable Sea Serpent

The sea monster was sighted in New England and Canada's Maritime Provinces until 1962, when all reports ended. Twenty-five years later, in May 1997, the sea monster reappeared off the coast of Newfoundland. Two fishermen saw what they thought were floating garbage bags. Planning to pick them up, they got within 60 feet when one of the bags lifted its head. The creature, which had the head of a horse, swiveled its six-foot-long neck and studied them. Then it sank beneath the waves.

In 1982, a video surfaced in the Chesapeake Bay area. The creature shown appeared in shallow water about 200 feet from the shore. It was dark in color, many humped, and about one foot in diameter. Since then there have been a constant stream of stories, photos, and videotapes from both Maryland and Virginia. Researchers at the Smithsonian Institution think the pictures and films show a living animal. No one, though, can identify what it is. One thing that the reports have in common is that they all describe characteristics of the monster from Gloucester.

The sea serpent of Gloucester may not be a serpent, a prehistoric whale, or a reptile. What we do know is that something returns year after year to fish off the Atlantic coast.

THE CADBOROSAURUS

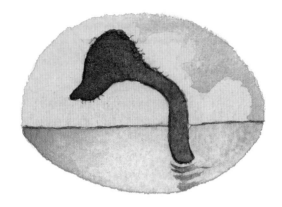

It was February 1934 and Cyril and Norman had just begun a day of hunting along the shore of Pender Island, not far from Vancouver, British Columbia. When the first duck they shot fell into the water, they climbed into their boat and paddled out to retrieve it. Just as they approached the duck, something exploded from the water. Although it was only 10 feet away, they could only identify a head and two segments, or loops, of a body. Then it opened its mouth. With razor-sharp teeth, it snatched the duck and gulped it down. Cyril and Norman couldn't believe what they had seen. Its head was like a horse's, but it had no ears. Its body was like that of a snake, but it could rise several feet up out of the water. Its color was a greyish-brown. It wouldn't be the last time they saw Caddy.

Later that year they had another round with the sea monster. Once again, the hunters were on their way to retrieve a fallen duck. This time two monsters appeared to steal their prize. As one of the creatures gulped down the duck, they noted the size of its head. It looked to be about six feet long. Cyril called for help. A justice of the peace and several others rushed to the shore. They saw one of the creatures swim away. Even though it was 20 yards out, they estimated it to be about 40 feet long and at least 2 feet in diameter.

The Creature: A Monster with a Mustache?

Many people saw the sea monster along the coast of North America. His favorite spot seemed to be Cadboro Bay in British Columbia. He was spotted there so many times that he was nicknamed after the bay. His full name was the cadborosaurus, but fans called him Caddy.

Caddy was said to be dark brown, steel gray, or black. Scientists agreed that the description sounded as if he came from a family of vertebrates, animals that have a backbone. He seemed both a reptile and a mammal. Like a whale and all other mammals, he had hair, a horizontal tail that moved him up and down in the water, and eyes that reflected light. Being long and snakelike, he resembled a reptile.

Observers said the monster had a scaly back with muscles that moved like a python's. This represented a problem for scientists. The narrow body couldn't possibly hold heat in the cold waters of the Pacific. Mammals living in the deep ocean were big and round, such as whales, seals, and manatees. What was Caddy?

Guesses of Caddy's size varied. The monster's length was estimated at between 30 and 100 feet. His skull was wide and diamond shaped. To some it looked similar to the head of a horse, giraffe, or camel.

It resembled a snake's head to others. Some observers said his lips were full and pale. Others saw whiskery hairs bristling in a mustache that stretched across his face. Underneath the mustache they saw sharp, needlelike teeth.

Caddy's long, thick neck was between 3 and 12 feet long. Down the back of his neck was a series of humps. Some speculated that the humps were tufts of hair, others said they were part of his body. Ivan Sanderson, a nature writer, thought the humps were a type of breathing mechanism that helped Caddy gather oxygen for long stays underwater. Those who speculated that the humps were part of its body supposed they were used for balance in the water.

Caddy's bulging eyes were a foot in diameter. They were black but reflected light, so could look red or green. Reports said the eyes looked sometimes sad, sometimes frightening. Still others felt the eyes were friendly. Everyone agreed on the usefulness of its large eyes for life in the deep. If the monster fed on the bottom of the ocean floor, it would need big eyes to collect light. This led scientists to speculate that Caddy lived in the twilight world of deep water.

Scientists also guessed Caddy swam alone. Since he had to eat large amounts of fish to support his size, he needed a big hunting ground. Would mating be a problem? Solitary hunters solve that problem by coming together for mating season. Also, since each creature's territory was close to another's, mating might not be a problem. In the winter months, they would all travel to deep water, and in the summer, the females would come to shore to give birth.

Since Caddy didn't have the big mouth of a shark or whale, it had to be fast to catch prey. One couple, driving along the Oregon coast, had to travel at twenty-five miles per hour to match the speed of the Caddy they tracked. When two float planes landed next to a pair of cadborosauruses, the monsters swam away at a speed of sixty-five miles per hour.

Fact or Fancy: From Cave to Camera, Pictures Exist

Caddy has been around the Pacific Northwest for a long time. Images of a long-necked sea monster have appeared on cave walls and in crafts and legends.

There is a wooden spear, over 1,700 years old, at the University of British Columbia that depicts the image of a sea monster. In 1937, a baby cadborosaurus was said to have been snared in a fisherman's net and preserved for over three weeks. (After which a museum director tossed it out.) That same year, a strange-looking skeleton was found in the body of a sperm whale. The fishermen had laid the skeleton out on a dock and photographed it. It had a horse-shaped skull, a snakelike body, and a humped back. Since the skeleton was only 10 feet long, it was guessed to be a baby cadborosaurus.

Scientists have been divided on the subject of Caddy. Some say giant turtles and porpoises cause the moving bumps on the water. Others think people are spotting giant sharks. In fact, a few decided the skeleton found in the sperm whale was a basking shark, not a monster. Sharks have skeletons made mostly of soft cartilage, not bone. When one dies, large portions of cartilage rot away quickly, leaving a carcass that might look like a cadborosaurus.

Spotting Caddy in the water could be explained by studying the action of waves. Wave motion makes logs appear to splash, almost as if they are living creatures.

Also, the waves at sea move in one direction, which makes the object seem to move in the other direction.

A question always asked by cynics is "Why haven't people seen evidence of Caddy along the Pacific coast?" After all, most ocean animals are washed up on the beaches. If Caddy exists, wouldn't bones remain? Believers say Caddy would wriggle off the beach like a seal, so he would never beach like a whale. Once in the water, the remains would be eaten by sea creatures or dissolved by sea water.

Another speculation is that Caddy is an oarfish, also called a ribbonfish. This ocean creature looks like a sea serpent and has large, saucerlike eyes. One oarfish measured over 44 feet and another weighed over 600 pounds. The oarfish is rarely seen because it lives in the deeps and only comes to the surface if it is sick or injured. An oarfish is silver and has a crest on its back and head that is bright red and, like Caddy, the oarfish has large saucerlike eyes. But those who see the bright color of the oarfish, believers argue, would not mistake it for a cadborosaurus.

Oarfish, basking shark, even a conger eel might explain some of the reports of Caddy. Yet fans ask doubters to consider the unexplored territory of the

ocean floor. About a quarter million marine species have been detected and classified. Some say there are several more million awaiting discovery.

Recent Sightings: Caddy Just Won't Go Away

The year 1997 was a good one for cadborosaurus watching. One July day, two university students took time to enjoy the summer weather. About 50 feet from where they perched, a snorting creature broke the waves. It surfaced once more before it disappeared under the water. The creature reminded them of a whale, but it didn't spray as it came out of the water. Also, it had at least two humps, unlike the whale. They guessed it to be about 20 feet long. When they reported their findings to a retired cryptozoologist at the Royal British Columbia Museum, Dr. Edward L. Bousfield, he said they had probably seen a cadborosaurus.

In August of the same year, a British Columbia family had two encounters with a cadborosaurus. They were sailing up an inlet when a big log suddenly appeared in their path. As they passed the log, it broke in three pieces and disappeared into a swirling whirlpool. They didn't think much about it until later that month when they saw something extraordinary. An object in the water was leaving behind an odd trail. Curious, the mother raised her binoculars for a closer look. She saw a creature swimming like a snake. Dr. Bousfield thought they had seen a female cadborosaurus. He theorized that the creature, like any female reptile, was going to shore to give birth.

Dr. Bousfield and oceanographer Paul LeBlond studied hundreds of cadborosaurus reports and believed some of them to be real. They presented their evidence to zoologists and published a book, *Cadborosaurus: Survivor of the Deep.* Many others shared their belief. In fact, in May 2003, the city of Oak Bay, British Columbia, initiated a Caddy Watch. A reward of ten thousand dollars was offered to anyone who could bring in a three-minute authentic videotape.

Even though no one has claimed the prize, fans aren't discouraged. It took nine centuries for the existence of a colossal squid to be verified by film. Since Caddy has yet to have an authentic photograph, they ask everyone to carry a camera and be quick with a click.

Experience has taught us that nature can be startling. Just as the discovery of the giant squid proves some sightings true, future discoveries may confirm reports of the monsters described in this book. Skepticism is healthy, but so is an open mind. One thing is certain: breakthroughs will be made. Which of these creatures might be among them?

Selected Resources

Books

Blackman, W. Haden. *The Field Guide to North American Monsters.* New York: Three Rivers Press, 1998.

Bord, Janet, and Colin Bord. *Unexplained Mysteries of the 20th Century.* New York: McGraw Hill, 1970.

Carrington, Richard. *Mermaids & Mastodons, a Book of Natural & Unnatural History.* New York: Rinehart & Co., Inc., 1957.

Clarke, Jerome. *Encyclopedia of Strange and Unexplained Physical Phenomena.* Farmington Hills, MI: Gale Group, 1993.

Cohen, Daniel. *America's Very Own Monsters.* New York: Dodd, Mead and Company, 1982.

———. *A Modern Look at Monsters.* New York: Dodd, Mead and Company, 1970.

Coleman, Loren. *Cryptozoology A to Z: The Encyclopedia of Loch Monsters, Sasquatch, Chupacabras, and other Authentic Mysteries of Nature.* New York: Simon and Schuster, 1999.

———. *Mysterious America.* London and Boston: Faber & Faber, 1983.

Dinsdale, Tim. *Monster Hunt.* Washington, DC: Acropolis Books, 1972.

Floyd, E. Randall. *Great Southern Mysteries.* Little Rock, AR: August House, 1991.

Heuvelmans, Bernard. *In the Wake of Sea-Serpents.* New York: Hill and Wang, 1968.

———. *On the Track of Unknown Animals.* New York: Hill and Wang, 1959.

Hunter, Don, and René Dahinden. *Sasquatch/Bigfoot.* New York: Firefly Books, 1993.

Keel, John A. *The Mothman Prophecies.* New York: Saturday Review Press, E. P. Dutton and Company, 1975.

Krantz, Grover. *Big Foot-prints: A Scientific Inquiry into the Reality of Sasquatch.* Boulder, CO: Johnson Books, 1992.

Mackal, Roy P. *Searching for Hidden Animals.* Garden City, NY: Doubleday and Company, 1980.

Morgan, Elaine. *The Descent of Woman.* New York City: Bantam Books, 1972.

Napier, John. *Bigfoot: The Yeti and Sasquatch in Myth and Reality.* New York: E. P. Dutton and Company, 1977.

Newton, Michael. *Monsters, Mysteries, and Man.* Reading, MA: Addison-Wesley, 1979.

Shuker, Karl P. N. *In Search of Prehistoric Survivors: Do Giant 'Extinct' Creatures Still Exist?* London: Blandford, 1999.

Web Sites

Natural History Museum:
http://www.nhm.ac.uk/nature-online/life/dinosaurs-other-extinct-creatures/index.html

British Broadcasting Company Site:
SCIENCE AND NATURE:
http://www.bbc.co.uk/sn/prehistoric_life/index.shtml

British Columbia Folklore Site:
http://www.info@folklore.bc.ca

Discovery.com:
http://www.discovery.com/

Dinosauria On-line:
http://www.dinosauria.com/

The Mysterious and the Unexplained:
   http://www.activemind.com/Mysterious

Natural Resources and Environmental Conservation: Snakes:
   http://www.umass.edu/nrec/snake_pit/pages/myth.html

The Cryptozoologist:
   http://www.lorencoleman.com/

Bigfoot Researcher's Organization:
   http://www.bfro.net/

ACKNOWLEDGMENTS

Thanks to my other family—my buddies at Anderson's Bookshop.

Thanks to other children, Mike Bernard, AJ Pebler, and Vigit Mohedeen, who inspired this book; the kids at Washington, Lincoln, and Kennedy Junior High who edited and improved it; and the students of the Clearmont and Burnsville Schools who want another one.

Thanks to Christy Ottaviano, who teaches me gently.